POLLY PIG and THE BEE

BY LUCY KINCAID

ILLUSTRATED BY PAMELA STOREY

BRIMAX BOOKS · NEWMARKET · ENGLAND

Polly Pig wants some
sweets. There are no
sweets in the jar. Polly Pig
likes sweets.
"I will go to the shop,"
says Polly Pig. "I will buy
some more sweets."
The bee likes sweets. "I
will go to the shop with
Polly Pig," says the bee.

Polly Pig puts on her hat.
She is ready to go.
Polly Pig shuts the door.
The bee is outside.
"Go away bee," says Polly Pig.
"Buzz!" says the bee. "I want some sweets."
"There are no sweets," says Polly Pig. "Go away!"

Polly Pig goes down the hill. She sees Bob Hedgehog.
''Where are you going?'' says Bob Hedgehog.
''To the shop to buy some sweets,'' says Polly Pig.
''I will buy some too,'' says Bob Hedgehog. ''Can I go with you?''
''Yes, you can,'' says Polly Pig.

The bee goes after them.
"Go away bee," says Polly Pig.
"What does the bee want?" says Bob Hedgehog.
"Buzz!" says the bee. "I want some sweets."
"We have no sweets," says Bob Hedgehog. "Go away."
The bee buzzes. The bee is cross.

Little Hamster is sitting on the fence.
"Where are you going?" says Little Hamster.
"To the shop, to buy some sweets," says Polly Pig.
"I will buy some too," says Little Hamster. "Can I come with you?"
"Yes, you can," says Polly Pig.

Little Hamster gets down from the fence. They all go along the road. The bee goes too.

"Go away bee," says Polly Pig.

"What does the bee want?" says Little Hamster.

"Buzz!" says the bee. "I want some sweets."

"We have no sweets," says Little Hamster. "Go away."

They go into the shop.
They shut the door. The
bee is outside. Cheepy
Chick is in the shop.
"What do you want?" says
Cheepy Chick.
"I want to buy some
sweets," says Polly Pig.
"So do I," says Bob
Hedgehog.
"So do I," says Little
Hamster.

The shop is full of jars. The jars are full of sweets. There are yellow ones, brown ones, white ones, pink ones and green ones. "Which sweets do you want?" says Cheepy Chick.

"I will have yellow
sweets," says Polly Pig.
Cheepy Chick goes up the
ladder. She gets the jar.
She brings it down. She
puts some sweets in a bag.
"I will have green sweets,"
says Bob Hedgehog.
"I will have white sweets,"
says Little Hamster.

Polly Pig pays for her sweets.
Bob Hedgehog pays for his sweets.
Little Hamster pays for his sweets.
The bee is looking at them.
"Will that be all?" says Cheepy Chick.
"Yes, thank you," they say.
"Goodbye," says Cheepy Chick. She opens the door.
"Come again," says Cheepy Chick.

The bee is waiting.
"Go away bee," says Polly Pig.
"Buzz!" says the bee. "I want some sweets."
"Go away," says Bob Hedgehog.
"Buzz!" says the bee. "I want some sweets".
"Go away," says Little Hamster.
"Buzz!" says the bee. "I want some sweets."

"You cannot have any of my sweets," says Polly Pig.
"You cannot have any of my sweets," says Bob Hedgehog.
"You cannot have any of my sweets," says Little Hamster.
"Please," buzzed the bee.
"Please, can I have some sweets?"

"Yes, now you have said 'Please', that is the proper way to ask," says Polly Pig. "I will give you some sweets."

Bob Hedgehog gives the bee some sweets.

Little Hamster gives the bee some sweets.

The bee says, "Thank you!
Thank you!
Thank you!"

Say these words again

buy
buzzes
sitting
waiting
outside
please
ready

goes
jars
goodbye
thank you
which
pays
again